The Goffins
Go Batty

The Goffins
Go Batty

JEANNE WILLIS
illustrated by **Nick Maland**

WALKER
BOOKS

For Leon, who arrived like the cavalry.
J.W. Plot 74b.
J.W.

For Brian and Johan with Love
N.M.

First published 2010 by Walker Books Ltd
87 Vauxhall Walk, London SE11 5HJ

2 4 6 8 10 9 7 5 3 1

Text © 2010 Jeanne Willis
Illustrations © 2010 Nick Maland

The right of Jeanne Willis and Nick Maland to be identified as
author and illustrator respectively of this work has been asserted by them
in accordance with the Copyright, Designs and Patents Act 1988

This book has been typeset in ITC Veljovic

Printed and bound in Great Britain by Clays Ltd, St Ives plc

British Library Cataloguing in Publication Data:
a catalogue record for this book is available from the British Library

ISBN 978-1-4063-0871-6

www.walker.co.uk

CONTENTS

THE CARRUTHERS

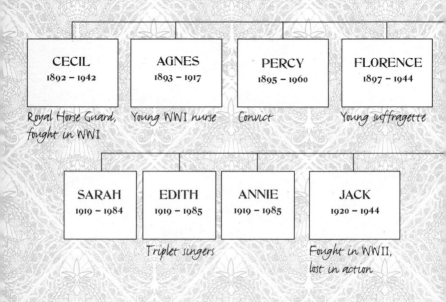

CECIL	AGNES	PERCY	FLORENCE
1892 – 1942	1893 – 1917	1895 – 1960	1897 – 1944

Royal Horse Guard,   Young WWI nurse   Convict   Young suffragette
fought in WWI

SARAH	EDITH	ANNIE	JACK
1919 – 1984	1919 – 1985	1919 – 1985	1920 – 1944

Triplet singers

Fought in WWII,
lost in action

FAMILY TREE

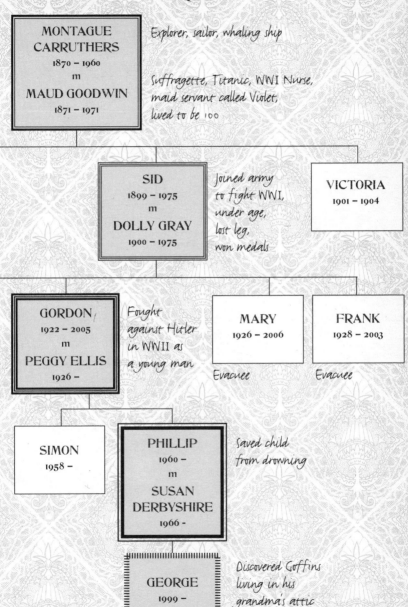

MONTAGUE CARRUTHERS
1870 – 1960
m
MAUD GOODWIN
1871 – 1971

Explorer, sailor, whaling ship

Suffragette, Titanic, WWI Nurse, maid servant called Violet, lived to be 100

SID
1899 – 1975
m
DOLLY GRAY
1900 – 1975

Joined army to fight WWI, under age, lost leg, won medals

VICTORIA
1901 – 1904

GORDON
1922 – 2005
m
PEGGY ELLIS
1926 –

Fought against Hitler in WWII as a young man

MARY
1926 – 2006

Evacuee

FRANK
1928 – 2003

Evacuee

SIMON
1958 –

PHILLIP
1960 –
m
SUSAN DERBYSHIRE
1966 –

Saved child from drowning

GEORGE
1999 –

Discovered Goffins living in his grandma's attic

CHAPTER ONE

BUBBIES AND BINOCKLES

Something had woken George. Unable to get back to sleep, he tugged the cord on the blind and opened it a little. It was still dark outside. As he lay gazing at the stars through the attic window of Grandma Peggy's house, for the first time he felt like it was his house too. He realized he wasn't homesick any more.

When he'd first moved from London with his mum and dad, he'd hated living at his grandma's. Being an only child he'd missed his old friends, but things were looking up.

The kids at his new school were OK. He still felt a bit of an outsider but in many ways he was glad about that. If he had a best friend, he might let his secret slip and he'd promised Lofty and Eave he'd never tell a soul that they existed.

Eave was like the little sister George had always hoped for and Lofty was the kind of father he wanted his own dad to be. But there was something else that made Lofty and Eave fifty times more fun than anyone he'd ever met before: they were Goffins.

According to Lofty, the Goffins were a forgotten race of people whose tiny island sank into the Irish Sea centuries ago. Their ancestors had escaped in boats and as no one would give them house-room, they made themselves at home in the tops of abandoned buildings where, unbeknownst to Them Below, they'd been bringing up their families ever since.

George was dying to tell someone there were Goffins living in his grandma's attic but he'd promised not to. It would have made life so much easier if his mum was in on the secret because then she wouldn't keep asking where all the biscuits had gone. Or the cake. Or the milk. Lofty and Eave struggled to survive on the fruit and vegetables they grew on the roof but George could hardly admit he stole food for them. If anyone knew the Goffins existed, they'd have to move out and that was the last thing George wanted.

Just then, George realized what had woken him up. He could hear somebody or something whimpering – there it was again! It seemed to be coming from behind the small green door opposite his bed – the door that led to the home Lofty and Eave had furnished with the bric-a-brac stored by George's relatives over the generations.

Maybe the whimpering sound was Eave crying. George knew how much she missed her mother and her brother, Arch. If only he could take her to visit them in the church belfry where they lived with her Granny Cloister – but it was impossible. Goffins only travelled after dark in case they were seen, and he had no idea when the buses stopped running.

The whimpering was getting louder, and the louder it got, the less it sounded like a little girl in distress. Maybe it was Lofty playing a traditional Goffin tune on his twigaloo. Sometimes he played the twigaloo for fun, but he had been known to sit outside on the roof and use the curious hand-carved instrument to lure birds and animals by mimicking their calls.

If it was Lofty, it was most unlike him to risk waking Them Below by playing at such volume. He was usually very careful – except on the rare occasions when he opened the rum he'd discovered in a sailor's trunk that once belonged to George's great-great-grandpa, Montague Carruthers.

George put on his slippers and decided to investigate. His father had banned him from entering the loft in case he put a foot through the plaster and fell through the ceiling, but his dad had no idea how carefully furnished the loft really was. Lofty had laid old off-cuts of lino and carpet over the rafters and painstakingly arranged the long-forgotten furniture to form separate rooms, including a sitting room, two bedrooms, a bathroom and a kitchen.

These were decorated with all sorts of curiosities that Great-Great-Grandpa Monty had brought back from his wild trips abroad – all of which were recorded in a battered leather almanac that Eave had found in the same chest that held, among other things, the rum.

The keyhole to the attic door was blocked from the inside to prevent prying eyes, so

The Goffins Go Batty

George peered through a split in the timber
to see if Lofty and Eave were up and about. It
was pitch black inside. The chandelier, which
normally lit the place with wobbly, hand-
made candles, had been snuffed out. George
tapped on the door, using the agreed code
so that they'd know it was him – *pom ... tiddy
pom pom ... pom pom!*

There was no reply, so he tried again.
Just as he got to the last pom, he heard soft
footsteps. Slowly, the door creaked open.
Eave appeared out of the gloom,
rubbing her gooseberry
green eyes. She
was holding a tea
light in a gravy
boat and in
the soft glow
of the flame,
she looked
like a small,
sleepy spook.

"Jowge?" she yawned. "Myneself be a-sleepin! Whyfor be yourself awake?"

She tucked a copper coil of hair back under her bulbous, frilly nightcap, which had clearly once belonged to someone with a bigger head. She ushered George inside and slipped back into the darkness, only to be stopped short when George accidentally stood on the back of the tattered white gown trailing behind her like a bride's train. There was a ripping sound. Eave whipped round.

"Fi! Yourself be stompin' on myne besterly nightlie!"

George apologized after a fashion.

"Your best nightie? It looks ancient!"

"Yay, 'tis Violet's," she frowned.

Violet had been his Great-Great-Grandma Maud's servant. A while back, Eave had pointed her out to George on a sepia photograph – one of hundreds of pictures of his ancestors that she'd hung around the attic. Violet used to sleep in what was now his room, probably in the same nightdress Eave was now wearing. She plucked at the torn hem angrily.

"'Twas survivin' over a hundred summers till yourself did come a-stompin on it with normous slippins!"

Eave rarely got cross with George, so when she kicked him in the leg, it took him by complete surprise and he let out a sharp yell.

"Ow!"

Immediately, Lofty appeared from behind a life-sized wooden carving of an African king and began shushing him frantically.

"Jowge! Be yourself forgettin' us does live in dread of bein' cotched?"

George rubbed his shin and winced. "Hark who's talking!" he said. "If you're so afraid of being caught, what's with all the whimpering? I bet that was you out on the roof playing your twigaloo!"

Lofty shook his head so hard, his nightcap span around 360 degrees. He thrust his hands into the pockets of the purple, quilted smoking jacket he wore as a dressing gown and turned them inside out to prove that they were empty.

"Nay, 'twas never! A rowdy Goffin be rarer than a boggyman's belch. That whumperin' sound be a hound a-weepin. 'Tis oh-nee a littley, be-sounds of it."

17

"Really?" said George. "You reckon it's a stray puppy?"

Eave's eyes lit up. "Yay! A houndbubby! Myneself be lovin' one of those. Pappy, can us be keeping it? Oh Pappy, myneself be gaggin' for a hound. Please be sayin' yay!"

Her eyes were brimming with fake tears. If any other girl had done that it would have annoyed George, but for some reason he could forgive Eave just about anything. After all, she was – or so she fondly called herself – his step-in sister.

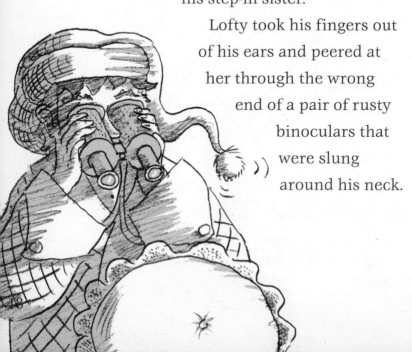

Lofty took his fingers out of his ears and peered at her through the wrong end of a pair of rusty binoculars that were slung around his neck.

"Alack, 'spite much searchin' through these trusty binockles and 'spite leanin' off the roof at a most rakish angle, myneself be failin' to be-scover the whereabouts of yonder houndbubby."

Eave thought for a moment, then grabbed George by the shoulders, braced both feet on his unsuspecting knees and hauled herself up until their noses were pressed together. She smiled at him hopefully.

"Jowge? Myneself is most sorry for the swift kickin'. If yourself be truly myne best step-in brother, yourself will be-fetch us the houndbubby."

If only he could. George had always wanted a dog, but for many reasons his dad wouldn't let him have one. If there was a stray puppy outside he'd love to bring it up to the loft and share it with Lofty and Eave, but what would they feed it on?

Dogs needed meat and biscuits to stay healthy. They could live on scraps but George always gave any leftovers to Lofty and Eave or they'd go hungry. He wouldn't be able to save enough food to feed a growing puppy too.

And what about vet bills? His pocket money would never stretch to that.

Also, dogs needed to go for walks or they made puddles indoors. How was he supposed to sneak a puppy in and out without his parents spotting it? And it was bound to bark.

George sighed. "It would never work, Eave. It's hard enough keeping you a secret, never mind a dog."

Her face fell, she let go of George and turned her back on him.

"Jowge be sayin' the truth, Littley," said Lofty. "Be thankly yourself has Chimbley to coddle."

Chimbley was Eave's pet pigeon. She lived in a pie dish up in the rafters and provided them with eggs all year round.

21

"And you've got Roofus,' added George. "I know he's only a squirrel but he's very tame and he fetches you fruit and nuts and stuff, which a dog would never do."

But there was no consoling Eave. She turned and walked off slowly in the direction of her bedroom, clutching her chest and muttering to herself.

"Oh, woe! Myne houndless heart be full of miseree! Myneself be goin' back to bed ... for *evertimes*!"

George knew she wasn't as upset as she made out, but even so, he wanted to make her happy.

"Wait!" he said. "There might be a way."

CHAPTER TWO

SAUSAGES AND SQUIRRELS

"Mum, can I have a dog?"

George's mum threw her coat on over her nurse's uniform and ignored him, so he tried again.

"Mum ... *please* can I have a dog?"

"Why must you do this to me now, George? I'm late for work already."

George blocked her path to the front door. "Mum, at least think about it, yeah?"

"I have," she said. "And I've got enough to do looking after Grandma."

Grandma Peggy was quite hard work. She was going deaf, she couldn't climb the stairs, and, try as she might, she couldn't manage on her own – not since Grandpa Gordon died. That's why they'd had to move in with her.

Grandma could be very cantankerous, but then so could George. In many ways, they were alike, and after a rocky start they had become allies. He had a feeling she knew about the Goffins. He also suspected that she knew he knew about them too, but neither of them would admit it to the other.

"Mum, I'll help you look after Grandma," insisted George. If it meant he could have a dog, there wasn't much he wouldn't do. She ruffled his hair and dashed out.

"Great! Could you hang her washing out please?"

This wasn't quite the result George had been hoping for. His plan had been to get his mother to agree to having a dog so that *she* could persuade his dad – something George could never do on his own. Then he'd find the stray puppy and give his parents such a sob story, it would be impossible for them to turn it away without looking completely heartless.

But now with his hopes dashed, he sloped off to take Grandma's wet washing out of the machine. He was in a bad mood now. He didn't think it was his job to hang out the clothes – that's what mothers were for – but then he remembered how shocked Eave had been when he told her he didn't do any housework.

Goffin children always helped with the chores. It was a matter of necessity. They had no electricity, so they had no washing machines, no ovens, no vacuum cleaners.

Everything had to
be done by hand. They
had to learn how to make
fires without matches so they
could cook. They had no money and
couldn't go the shops, so they had to grow
their own food, find it or fish for it from the
roof. Life was tough for Goffins.

As George lugged the dripping laundry
into the garden, he realized that actually,
he had things very easy. Offering to do a bit
more around the house wouldn't hurt him.
It might even convince his parents that he
wasn't too lazy to look after a dog.

As he pegged Grandma's enormous knickers on the line, he fantasized about the lost puppy. If only he could find it and keep it, how happy Eave would be. When no one was around, he'd take it into the loft and she could play with it and pet it and brush it and—

"That's no way to peg things, boy!" said Grandma.

Her room was on the ground floor facing the garden and she'd struggled out through the French windows with her walking frame to see what he was up to.

29

"You're getting creases in my smalls," she complained.

If these were Grandma's smalls, George would hate to see her larges. Under her strict instructions, he turned them inside out to get the air to them and pegged them by the waistband instead of the gusset.

"You've got a funny look on your face," said Grandma. "What are you thinking?"

"I'm thinking there's enough elastic in your pants to mend my catapult," said George. "Can I have them?"

"No, you can't! Flamin' cheek."

But he could see she was hiding a smile. She told him she'd got some spare elastic in her needlework box if he was desperate, so he walked back down the garden path with her. She was so slow, he had to take really small steps so that he didn't get ahead of her.

"That's a silly way to walk, boy. You should join the army. That'll put hairs on your chest."

George pointed out that as he was still at junior school, he was a bit too young to be a soldier.

"So was your Grandpa Gordon," she said, "but that didn't stop him. He fought Hitler in the Second World War."

"Who won?" asked George.

Grandma tutted loudly. "Don't they teach you anything at school?"

31

History wasn't exactly his best subject. He'd never been interested in the past before – he thought it didn't concern him. But since he'd met Eave, he'd learnt all sorts about the history of his own family. Having gone through all the old papers, documents and diaries stashed away in the attic, Eave had managed to trace George's family tree going back to his Great-Great-Grandparents. She'd even shown him *his* name, right at the bottom, waiting for his own story to be told.

George helped Grandma back indoors.

"I didn't know about Grandpa Gordon, but I knew Great-Grandpa Sid was a soldier in the First World War," he said. "He won a medal for bravery, didn't he?"

"Who told you that then, your dad?"

"Yep," he lied. "We often talk about these things."

George and his dad weren't exactly close – at least they hadn't been until George met Lofty. Lofty had a great deal of time for

George and when George complained that his own father took no interest in him, Lofty said that these things worked both ways; George could start by taking some interest in his father.

Usually, George never listened to his dad long enough for him to finish a sentence. Recently, though, he'd been making more of an effort to talk to him – but he still wasn't sure if his dad liked dogs.

George thought Grandma was probably the best person to ask, given that she was his father's mother, but her reply was somewhat strange.

"Does he like dogs? What's that got to do with the price of fish?"

"I really want a dog," said George, "and I was wondering if you could persuade him to let me have one."

Grandma didn't reply. She handed him the elastic and sat down in her chair with a loud "oof!" It was a sound she always made when she got in or out of a chair. She said it was because her legs hurt, but George had caught her dancing once when she thought he wasn't looking. He went to shut the French windows but she flapped her hands at him.

"Leave them open, boy. Then I can feed the squirrels. There's a nice fat grey one with a bushy tail that comes right in ... oh, here he is."

It was Roofus. George recognized him immediately and by the looks of him, Roofus recognized George – he'd fed him by hand the first time Eave had led him, shaking, onto the roof. Much to Eave's amusement, George still hadn't conquered his fear of heights.

Grandma snapped a biscuit in half.

"Here, throw him a bit of gingernut, boy. You'll never guess what he does with 'em."

George knew exactly what Roofus did with Grandma's biscuits – he took them to Eave. She'd trained him to do it.

"He stores them in his cheeks, runs up the wall and takes them right up to the roof," continued Grandma.

Roofus snatched the piece of gingernut from George and, as if to prove her point, he climbed up the ivy and disappeared over the top of the gutter.

"They eat sausages, you know," said Grandma.

"What ... squirrels?"

George was surprised. He was no naturalist, but even he knew that squirrels ate nuts and fruit. Surely they didn't eat meat?

"Well, somebody took my sausage," said Grandma. "I left it on my plate, went for a tiddle and when I came back, it had gone. If a squirrel didn't take it, who did, boy?"

35

George hesitated. The most likely explanation was that Lofty had snatched the sausage with his rod and hook. He went fishing from the roof most days. Sometimes he caught fruit and vegetables from the garden. Sometimes he caught crusts of bread left out for the birds and sometimes he cast his line further afield and trawled the pavement for treasure people had dropped: a box of matches, a bag of onions, a magazine with a free sachet of shampoo. It was amazing what he managed to haul in.

"Who pinched my sausage if it wasn't a squirrel?" repeated Grandma. She was watching George's expression carefully.

"Maybe a dog stole it," he said.

"What dog? I haven't seen one around here, have you, boy?"

"I heard one last night. It was whimpering, like it was lost and needed a good home."

"A word of advice," said Grandma. "Don't you go looking for trouble."

But George had already gone.

CHAPTER THREE

CARP
AND COLLARS

The puppy wasn't in the orchard at the bottom of the garden. Nor was it hiding behind the coal bunker. Nor was it asleep in the summer house. George searched all afternoon but he couldn't find it anywhere. Now he'd run out of places to look and was beginning to wonder if the puppy had ever existed in the first place.

He hated to disappoint Eave. He wanted to live up to her perfect big brother, Arch. Eave worshipped Arch; he was lion-brave. He'd never let her down. If she'd asked Arch to find the puppy, no doubt he'd have found the whole litter and let her take her pick.

George was about to go back to the
attic to break the bad news when he had a
brainwave. He could give Eave a goldfish out
of Grandma's pond. True, it wasn't the same
as a puppy, but it would be an easy thing to
keep. It wouldn't bark. It wouldn't need to go
for a walk every day and he could afford fish
flakes to feed it.

There was a old fishing net in the shed and
several jars full of nails and screws. He
chose the largest jar, tipped out the
contents and made his way to
the pond, which was hidden
from the house by a
willow tree.

There didn't seem
to be nearly as
many fish in there
as he remembered.
The large ones had
disappeared altogether.

Maybe they'd died of old age, like Grandpa Gordon. Luckily, there were still a few small ones hiding under the lily pads so he went after those.

Unluckily, the net was rotten. It was full of holes, so every time he caught a fish, it slithered back into the water. In the end, he decided to give up on the net and surprised himself by swooping a nice, fat goldfish straight into the jar at his first attempt.

Triumphant, he hid it under his jacket in case he bumped into Grandma, and made his way up to the attic. He knocked on the green door. *Pom ... tiddy pom pom ... pom pom!* There was a squeal of delight from the other side.

"Ooh, Pappy, 'tis Jowge. Darst say himself be fetchin' myne houndbubby!"

41

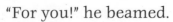

She let him in and
George held up the jar.
It was a particularly
pretty fish. He was sure
she'd love it.

"For you!" he beamed.

Eave didn't say a word. She gave him a
small, wobbly smile and, whisking away a tear,
she fled in the direction of their kitchen with
the jar. She was clearly disappointed. George
sat down on the battered chaise longue next to
Lofty and looked at him in despair.

"I did try to find the puppy."

Loftly gave him a manly squeeze.

"Darst say houndbubby be hidin' himself
someplace most hidden." He rubbed his belly.
"No matter, yourself be-fetchin' a tastefill
carp, for which us be truly thanklee!"

It took a few seconds for George to digest
what Lofty had just said.

"Oh no, you're not meant to eat it!" He
made a dash for the kitchen, only to find that

Eave had already set light to his great-great-grandpa's camping stove and was about to tip the goldfish into a pan of melted butter.

"Stop!" George grabbed the jar. Eave looked bemused.

"Whyfor Jowge? Doesn't yourself be likin' carp for dinnin's? 'Tis most tastefil."

"It's meant to be a pet! You're not meant to cook goldfish."

"Yay us is! Pappy is oftentimes fishin' for 'em."

No wonder there were so few left in the pond.

Eave folded her arms and sulked. "Now myneself has no dinnin's"

"Really?" said George. "Are you sure you haven't got sausages by any chance?"

Eave's gooseberry green eyes opened wider and wider.

"Sausagins?"

He glared at her accusingly.

"Grandma Peggy had a sausage on her plate at breakfast and when she turned her back, someone took it."

Eave shrugged innocently.

"'Twas yonder houndbubby, most likely."

"There is no puppy," said George. "If there was, I'd have brought it to you."

"But us did hear himself whumperin'!"

Maybe they'd all been mistaken. Or maybe the puppy had existed but was long gone. Either way, George felt like a failure.

"Sorry, Eave. It was a stupid idea, thinking you'd be happy with a goldfish. I'm working on getting a dog though. If I show Mum I can be trusted, maybe she'll let me have one and we can share him."

Eave wrung her apron and blushed.

"Shame on myneself. Yourself be most kind, givin' us a carp for pettin', Jowge. Myneself has Chimbley and Roofus too, yet yourself has none to love."

Lofty wandered in eating an apple riddled with holes. He sat down at the kitchen table and watched the goldfish swimming about in the jar. Eave sat on his lap.

"Jowge says us mustn't be eatin' it, Pappy. 'Tis a pet."

Lofty stopped chewing, pulled a face and spat a wriggling maggot into his fist. "Aha! Myne appil be havin' a visitor!" He dropped the maggot into the jar and the fish gobbled it up immediately.

"Every Goffin littley must be havin' a pet," he mused. "Howfor else be themselves learnin' about nurture?"

"Yeah," said George. "How can I learn to

look after a pet if no one lets me try?
I thought Grandma might get Dad to
let me have a dog but she said not
to go looking for trouble."

Eave tutted
sympathetically. "'Tis
most odd, considerin'
Grandmuppy Peg did
have a fine hound once-a-
times."

"How do you know
Grandma had a dog?"

Eave grabbed George's
hand. "Come see!"

She led him out of the
kitchen, past the bathroom
and along a corridor lined
with antique mirrors.
At the end, there was a
grandfather clock and
when she reached it, she
stopped.

"Here be myne boudoir, Jowge."

"Your bou...?"

"Where myneself do sleep."

The grandfather clock had no back to it; Lofty had hinged the front to a post – pendulum and all – and turned it into a door. This led to Eave's bedroom. George had often wondered what it looked like and it was even more bizarre than he'd imagined.

The far walls were made from huge, oriental rugs, which still bore the marks of the heavy chairs that had once stood on them, along with several stains that he guessed must be Victorian gravy.

The rest of the room was enclosed
by heavy curtains hung on brass rings
suspended from the attic beams. Over the top
of these, a false ceiling had been made from
several pairs of net curtains. These had been
stitched together and draped over the tops of
the rug-and-curtain walls where they hung in
drifts, like ivory clouds.

Against one of the walls was a child-sized
bed with a Mickey Mouse headboard. It
was more modern than the other pieces of
furniture but it was still pretty old.

"Come sit!" laughed Eave, patting the
eiderdown. "'Twas your Pappy Phillip's."

George sat down on his dad's old bed among a pile of china-faced dolls and balding teddy bears. As he did so, Eave disappeared under the bed. After a lot of scrabbling, she reappeared with a hat box trimmed with gold tassels. She took the lid off and tipped the contents onto the bed.

Among the necklaces, brooches and bracelets was a worn leather dog collar decorated with small brass studs. Eave pointed out the name engraved on the tarnished silver disc.

"See? Himself be called Rex."

George turned the collar over in his hands.

It would have fitted a small dog – a terrier maybe.

"How do you know he was Grandma Peggy's dog though?"

Eave went over to her dressing table and from behind a colourful collection of ribbons, hairbrushes and powder puffs she produced a faded photo of a girl in her late teens wearing an old-fashioned swimsuit. She was sitting on a beach with her arms around a dog who had a patch over one eye.

Both the dog and the girl seemed to be laughing. George smiled.

"That's Grandma Peggy?"

"Yay. Herself and Rex be havin' normous fun, nay?"

George lay back on the pillow and wished more than ever that he had a dog.

"Eave, how can I ever prove to Mum that I could look after one?" he sighed.

Just then, something fluttered in between the net ceiling and the curtain wall and crash-landed on the eiderdown.

It was a baby bat.

Chapter Four

FLIES AND FLUTTERMEECE

"Ah, 'tis a fluttermouse," said Eave, stroking the bat's orangey-brown fur.

"Is that the Goffin name for it?" asked George.

"Yay. Them Below be callin' himself a pipistrelle, but us be preferin' 'fluttermouse' 'cos himself be mouse-smincey and flutterin' most jerkilee."

George had never seen a bat in real life. Eave said she had seen plenty, but that was hardly surprising.

"Goffins and fluttermeece be sharin' the same dwellin's," she explained. "Both be likin' to roost in roofs. Oftentimes, myneself be seein' fluttermeece skimmin' over yonder pond afore sunsit. Themselves be sky-fishin', Jowge."

"What do they eat? Goldfish?"

"Nay," she said. "Fluttermeece be eatin' creepin-crawlin's, and flyin' gnits and moffs."

She blew softly on the bat's fur and when the fur parted, there was a wound on its chest.

"Fi, 'tis sorely!" whispered Eave. "Poor meece.

Darst say himself be-cotched by a pussen cat. Luckilee himself did escape, but us must be healin' him hastilee.'

There was a knock on her bedroom door. It was Lofty.

"'Tis rainin'," he said, "yet Grandmuppy Peg's washin' still be a-hangin' out."

George leapt up. "Argh! I forgot to bring it in. If Mum thinks I can't even look after the laundry, she'll never let me have a dog."

"Hastily, Jowge," said Eave. "Afore itself be soddin'. Myneself will be nursin' Gable."

"Gable?"

Eave held the tiny bat upside-down against her chest. "'Tis a goodly name for a fluttermouse, yay?"

Gable hooked his miniature claws into her clothes and gazed at her with boot button eyes. George had always imagined bats to be ugly creatures that got caught in girls' hair and sucked their blood, but Gable was nothing like that. He had a sweet face and delicate ears. George was amazed by the way his rubbery wings folded around him like an umbrella. He'd have stood and watched him all day if Eave hadn't interrupted.

"Hastily, Jowge, yourself be forgettin' the washin'! 'Tis dark already."

He squeezed himself back through the Grandfather Clock door and headed out of the attic. He hurried downstairs and ran into the garden with the laundry basket. The rain was easing off. He felt the washing; it wasn't too damp. If he was quick, he could finish drying it indoors before his mum got home.

It was only when he'd collected all the nylon socks and got to the middle of the washing

line that he noticed there was a gap between
the two nighties he'd pegged out earlier. An
item of clothing was missing.

"Pants!" shouted George.

Maybe they'd blown off the line – but how
could they? He'd pegged them out properly.
Grandma had stood there and watched him
to make sure of that. There was no doubt
about it: someone had nicked her knickers.
There was a lot of material in them, not to
mention elastic. A Goffin could make
very good use of those.

George looked up at the roof and was
certain he saw Lofty ducking down – he must
have been fishing for Grandma's underwear
the minute George's back was turned.

He was really embarrassed to ask, but he'd
have to go and get them back or Grandma
would be asking all sorts of awkward
questions. He took the laundry in, threw it
in the airing cupboard and ran back up the
three flights of stairs to the attic.

Pom ... tiddy pom pom ...
pom pom!

Lofty answered the
door with a startled
look on his face.

"Ha! You weren't
expecting me back
quite so quickly,
were you?" panted
George. "Come
on. Hand
them over!"

Lofty scratched his head quizzically. "Whatfor must myneself be handin'?"

George rocked on his heels like a policeman waiting for a confession.

"Come off it, Lofty. I know you've got Grandma Peggy's knickers."

Before George could stop him, Lofty undid the belt on the massive pair of explorer's shorts he was wearing and dropped them.

"Nay, myneself has not!"

As Lofty stood there in his baggy knitted long-johns, George averted his eyes.

"OK, if you're not wearing them, what have you done with them? If you needed elastic, I could have got you some. Grandma Peggy will go mad if she loses her pants."

59

Eave climbed back in through the skylight looking equally surprised to see George and even more surprised to see Lofty with his shorts around his ankles.

"Pappy! Whyfor be yourself showin' off your bloomin's?"

"Jowge be accusin' myneself of wearin' laydees clothin's!"

"I didn't!" exclaimed George.

He tried to explain the situation to Eave who insisted that neither she nor Lofty knew the whereabouts of the missing undies. George wasn't convinced.

"I saw you on the roof when I was in the garden. What were you doing if you weren't taking Grandma's knickers?"

"Tryin' to cotch moffs to be feedin' Gable," grumbled Lofty. He pulled up his shorts, produced a stubby candle from his pocket and waved it at George.

"Moffs be most attracted to candil-light, oh-nee the rain did put out myne flame.'

The excuse sounded so genuine, George was forced to admit that Lofty knew nothing about Grandma's missing knickers. Only one thing was puzzling him.

"Lofty, why were you trying to catch insects with a candle flame?" he asked. "You've got a torch. I gave you my old one – are the batteries dead?"

"Yay, themselves did pass away most sorrowfill sometime yesterly."

Eave stroked the little bat, which was still attached to her front like a furry brooch. His mouth kept opening and closing.

"Us must be feedin' Gable or himself will also be passin' away. If oh-nee myne brother Arch be here. Himself be swift at cotchin' moffs."

"You don't need Arch – I'm here now," said George, puffing out his chest. "I'm brilliant at catching insects. I'll get some from the

garden and feed Gable all through the night if
that's what it takes – how many does he need,
a couple of beetles and a slug?"

Eave counted slowly on her fingers, then
gave up.

"Himself needs about ... two hundrid
snackin's!"

"Two hun ... fine!" said George. "That's fine.
Give him to me. I'll look after him."

Eave seemed suitably convinced that he
could save the day. Very gently, she unhooked
Gable and helped
him get a grip on
George's jumper.

"Jowge be a Carruthers!" she announced to no one in particular. "Thus himself be handilin' beasts most skilfillee, like his Great-Great-Grandpappy Montague".

"Yep," said George.

He wished he had as much confidence in himself as Eave did, but actually he knew very little about caring for animals. Even worse, he'd hated insects ever since his so-called friend Dino stuffed a fistful of daddy-long-legs down his shirt at his old school in London.

There was nothing for it, he'd just have to conquer his fear, George told himself. His great-great-grandfather had fought polar bears and tigers; surely he could catch a few bugs without screaming like a girl. He put his shoulders back and steeled himself.

"I'll be off then!" he said, like a soldier going to war.

He'd fatten up Gable and get him well again. That would show everyone what he was capable of. Before he left, Eave reminded him of the bat's wound.

"Jowge? Be bathin' the soreness most regular with salty waters."

"Will do!"

He closed the attic door behind him and went to pick up the jacket he'd left on his bed.

"George! I thought Dad told you never to go in the loft."

He span round. His mum was standing in the doorway.

CHAPTER FIVE

REX AND RATIONS

"Don't ignore me, George!" said his mum. "What were you doing in the loft? Who were you talking to?"

"Gable," he grunted.

George lifted his left hand, which he'd been using to hide the fluttermouse.

"I was talking to my bat. I heard something flapping about. I opened the attic door and he just flew out... I didn't go inside." It was a lie, but he had to lie or his mother would start poking about in the attic and that would be the end of Lofty and Eave.

He cupped his hand back over the bat to

protect it – to stop her taking it from him. She
didn't even try; she sat down next to him on
the bed and her face softened.

"He's so sweet," she said.

George blew on Gable's fur like Eave had
done and showed her the wound.

"He's injured, Mum. I'm going to look after
him til he gets better. You can't stop me."

His mum examined the bat's tiny, pumping
chest as if he were one of her patients.

"That wants bathing in boiled, salty water,"
she said. "I'll put the kettle on."

When she left, Gable began to fidget and
flap his wings. He managed to escape for a
few seconds, fluttered crazily towards the
window and banged his head on the pane. He
fell with a sad plop into the waste bin. George
scooped him out, brushed
the coloured pencil
shavings out of his
fur and held him
close to his chest.

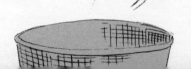

"I know it's night-time but you can't go yet, you're not well. I'll look after you."

His mum came back armed with cotton buds and salty water in a dish. She tested the temperature and began to dab at Gable's wound. George took the cotton bud from her.

"I'll do it. He's my bat."

"I can do it, George."

"So can I, Mum! I know you think I can't look after anything, but I can... Get off."

"Oh, but I wanted to..."

She let George do it but she was sulking. For a moment, she reminded George very much of Eave. He patted her hand.

"Tell you what, Mum. I'll let you cuddle my bat if you let me have a dog. Grandma won't mind, she loves dogs. She used to have one when she was a girl."

His mother frowned. "Grandma told you about Rex? That's odd, she's always refused to talk about him. Dad said never to mention his name in front of her in case she got too upset."

George felt queasy. Grandma hadn't told him about Rex – Eave had! He must be more careful when he opened his mouth. All he could do was let it pass and hope his mother never asked Grandma about the conversation they'd never had.

"Here, hold the baby," he said, hoping to get the attention away from himself.

She hooked the bat over the top pocket of her nurse's uniform and played with his ears.

George really wanted to ask why no one was allowed to talk about Grandma's dog, but without landing himself in it. What could have happened that was so terrible?

"She didn't say much about Rex," he said casually.

"She wouldn't. Your dad told me the story years ago, soon after we got married. It was

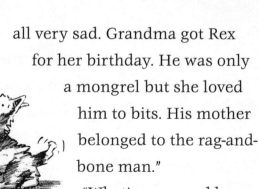

all very sad. Grandma got Rex for her birthday. He was only a mongrel but she loved him to bits. His mother belonged to the rag-and-bone man."

"What's a rag-and-bone man?" asked George.

"Oh, he used to go round with a horse and cart, collecting bones and old clothes to recycle. He'd ring a bell and yell, "Rag an' bo...ne! Rag an' bo...ne..."

She trailed off.

"Yeah, but what happened to Rex, did he get run over?'

"No, nothing like that. It was to do with the war. The government had to start rationing food. There wasn't enough meat in the shops for people, let alone dogs, so lots of pets had to be put to sleep."

George was shocked. "I'd never let anyone put my dog down. I'd have given it all my food!"

His mother looked at him fondly. "You might think differently if you had to live through a war, George. Grandma's dad was an old softy – he knew Rex ought to go but he couldn't bring himself to take him to the vet. So Peggy offered."

Only it seemed that Grandma was just as cunning then as she was now. The story went that she put Rex on his lead and pretended to take him to the vet – but didn't.

"Where did she take him, Mum?"

"She put him
in her bicycle
basket and
rode for miles
until she
came to a
wood. Then
she slipped off
his collar and lead and while he was busy
chasing rabbits, she rode off."

George sat there quietly. It had been such
a kind, heart-breaking thing for Grandma to
do. Part of him hoped that Rex had stopped
hunting, realized his mistress had gone and
followed her home.

"Did she ever see him again?"

"No. Goodness knows what happened to
him."

"But he could have survived on rabbits,
couldn't he? Lived to a good old age?"

"Or maybe someone found him and kept
him."

It would always be a mystery. They sat silently for a while, but then Gable started squeaking and opening his mouth again. George put his jacket on.

"I'll have to get him some insects. Have you got a box I could use to make him a cave? I was going to push a branch through it for him to hang on and put some leaves on the bottom in case he fell."

"Use the box Dad's PC came in. It's in the cupboard under the stairs, but George..."

"Hmm?"

"Try not to get too attached. Bats aren't easy to hand-rear. He might not survive."

George grabbed his goalie gloves and put them on. "He will if I have anything to do with it. You'll see."

He went to the kitchen to find something suitable to put the insects in. His dad was in there. He'd just got back from golf.

"What are you after now, George?"

"My school lunchbox."

"What do you want that for? It's the weekend."

"To put things in."

"What things?"

"Insects."

The lunchbox was trapped behind a pile of saucepan lids and when he pulled it, they fell out of the cupboard, span round the floor and fell over one by one with a series of loud crashes.

"Clumsy!" groaned his dad, chasing after the lids. "What do you want insects for?"

George held up the lunchbox.

"Here's a clue, Dad." It had a picture of Batman on the front, but his father clearly wasn't in the mood for guessing games, so George just ran outside with it.

He went down to the summer house. He'd seen several dead moths in there. If he managed to pick those up first, he could get over his phobia and go after some live ones.

Just as he got to the pond, he saw what he thought was bird flutter across the water, but as he stood and watched, he realized it was a bat. A pipistrelle like Gable, only bigger. Maybe it was his mother.

"It's okay," he said. "I promise I'll look after him, same as I promised Eave."

Saying that out loud made George feel even more determined and, gritting his teeth, he bent down to pick up a particularly slimy slug. It was the first of many and after two hours he had, by some miracle, managed to fill his lunch box almost to the top without gagging.

As he made his way back indoors with Gable's packed lunch, he hoped with all his heart that the little bat was still alive.

CHAPTER SIX

DOIN'S AND POOIN'S

George stayed up most of the night posting slugs, grubs and flies into Gable's ever-gaping mouth. It was only when the sun rose that the two of them finally fell asleep. Luckily, it was Sunday so he was able to have a lie-in. When he finally woke up, it was mid-day. He scratched his chest lazily and threw back his hand – there was something soggy on his pillow. It took him a moment to realize what it was – bat poo! With a sudden jolt, it reminded him he was meant to be in charge of Gable – but the bat seemed to have flown.

George scrambled out of bed – where was

he? Had he fallen asleep with him in his arms? Had he rolled on him and squashed him in the night? He flipped back the duvet – he wasn't there!

Then he remembered: he'd hung Gable up on a branch in the cardboard box cave. It was on the floor on the other side of the bed. With his mother's words ringing in his ears about not getting too attached, he knelt down to check that he was still alive.

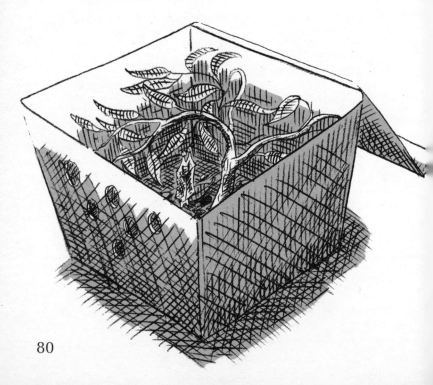

The bat was hanging upside down by his finger-claws, swaddled in his rubbery wings. His eyes were closed, but was he dead or alive? It wasn't easy to tell. George opened the blind. He watched for a while until he was sure Gable was breathing and heaved a sigh of relief.

"George!" came a cry from downstairs. "Do you want some lunch?" He hadn't even had his breakfast, so he threw some clothes on and went downstairs. His mum had made bacon and eggs, his favourite.

"Hey, George. How's Gable?"

George swallowed his bacon and yawned.

"He's asleep. He eats a lot. I was up most the night."

"It's a good sign if he's eating. I told Dad about him, by the way."

George pulled a face. "I'm not getting rid of him."

But George's dad had no intention of making him get rid of the bat.

"He thought it would teach you some responsibility," said his Mum. "He was very impressed with your bat cave. He saw it when he came in to say goodbye this morning, when you were asleep."

"Where's he gone? To see a man about a dog?"

"No, to visit Uncle Simon. He'll be back by dinner time. I've been asked to help out at the hospital jumble sale this afternoon – want to come? It'll be fun."

George couldn't think of anything less fun apart from double maths.

"I'd love to, but I can't. I've got to look after Gable."

His mother seemed impressed. "See the sacrifices you have to make when you have a pet, George? Will you be alright on your own?

"I won't be on my own, will I? I'll go and see the Gof..." He'd almost told her about Lofty and Eave again! He tried to cover his mistake.

"I said, "Go...I seem to have a cough."

He pretended to choke and spat out a piece of egg. His mother patted him on the back.

"Better? Who'd you say you were going to see, George?"

"Grandma."

He didn't go and see Grandma straight away though. As soon as his mum left to help out at the jumble sale he needed to see Lofty and Eave to tell them how Gable was doing. He grabbed the rest of the pint of milk, an almost-finished packet of cornflakes and the end of a loaf. Oh, and they needed batteries for the torch. He'd have taken them a piece of bacon but his mother had been watching him too closely at lunch to save any. He put everything in a bag and carried it up to the loft.

83

Eave was really excited to see him. At first he thought it was because she particularly liked cornflakes, but it wasn't that. It was far more exciting than that.

"Guess what?" She grabbed his hands and danced round.

"What?"

"Yesternights, Pappy be roof-fishin' for plums and suchlike when himself did say, "Lo! Does yourself be seein' what myneself is seein', Littley?'"

"And what did you see?" asked George.

"Myne houndbubby! Himself be squattin' Down Below on yonder lawn!"

Her eyes were sparkling. She dragged George to the far end of the attic, threw open the skylight and pointed past the lawn towards the orchard.

"Himself be out there hidin' someplace. Us must be lurin' and a-cotchin' him."

"How?"

Lofty came out of the kitchen with a sausage in his hand. He hadn't realized George was there, so quickly stuffed it back in his pocket and bowed deeply.

"Goodly Noon, Jowge. Howfor be young Gable?"

"He's fine," said George, pretending he hadn't seen the sausage. "He's asleep. I fed him insects all through the night and bathed his wound. I think it's scabbing over."

Lofty nodded approvingly. "'Tis a grand job yourself be doin'. Darst say us must be freein' him back into the wilders soontimes."

George's heart sank. He'd grown really fond of the little bat. He knew he'd have to let him go – it would be cruel not to – but he really wanted to keep him. Grandma must have felt like that about Rex, only worse – she'd had him for ten years.

"Did you know what happened to Rex, Lofty?"

"Nay, but us did wonder..."

So they all cuddled up on the battered chaise longue while George told them about the food rationing during the war and how young Peggy had saved Rex from a deadly trip to the vet.

When he'd finished the story, Eave dried
her eyes on her petticoat and disappeared
among the great bank of boxes and suitcases
into which she'd sorted his ancestors'
various belongings. When she returned,
she was clutching a booklet with a torn,
buff-coloured cover. She
showed it to George.

It was a ration book,
dated 8th January 1940. It had some coupons
left inside that showed how much food each
person in the family was allowed to have each
week: twelve ounces of sugar. Four ounces of
butter. Four ounces of bacon or ham.

It didn't sound much at all. George could easily eat a whole packet of bacon in one sitting. Lofty didn't see it that way though. He studied the ration book and seemed to think it was all very reasonable.

"'Tis plenty... Nay, tis a feast! Four oziz butter? Twelve oziz sugar? 'Tis more than us Goffins be gettin' yearly."

George suddenly realized how very greedy and over-fed he was compared to them. He didn't ever have to think about how much he ate – there was always plenty of food in the cupboard, and if they ran out they could always buy more.

But it hadn't been like that for his grandparents. Or his great-grandparents. And it had never been like that for the Goffins. They were on permanent rations though they were at war with no one. He decided to be even more generous with the food parcels he brought them in future.

"Look ... I got you some bread and milk too," he said, wishing now that he'd brought them a whole pint and a whole loaf instead of dregs and crumbs. They were so grateful for what little they got and so thrilled with the batteries, it made him feel guilty.

"Thanklee, Jowge! Such kindness. Whatever would us be doin' without yourself?"

"It's nothing. Really."

As Lofty and Eave tucked into their bread, milk and cereal, George announced that he was going off in search of the puppy.

"Darst say houndbubby will have left his callin' card!" smiled Lofty.

George didn't understand.

"His doin's an' pooin's," he explained.

Eave rapped him on the hand with her spoon.

"Pappy! 'Tis most foul to be speakin' of doin's and suchlike at us table!"

George grinned and let himself out of the loft, taking the goldfish with him – he'd decided to release it back into the pond. If Eave was that desperate for fish, he'd rather get her some cod from the chip shop.

He checked on Gable, who was still sleeping, then went out into the garden. He didn't find the puppy, but he did find the evidence that it had been there. In fact, he trod in it and had to spend the next half hour cleaning his trainers. Normally, the smell alone would have put him off, but overnight he'd become the kind of boy who could pick up slugs without screaming. The kind of boy who could sleep with bat poo on his pillow. A little bit of dog muck was no problem to a boy like that.

Where on earth was that puppy? As he cleaned his trainer treads with a stick, he kept constant watch in case the dog came lolloping out of the rhododendrons. It didn't though, so he decided to visit Grandma Peggy.

She was bound to have seen it, knowing her.

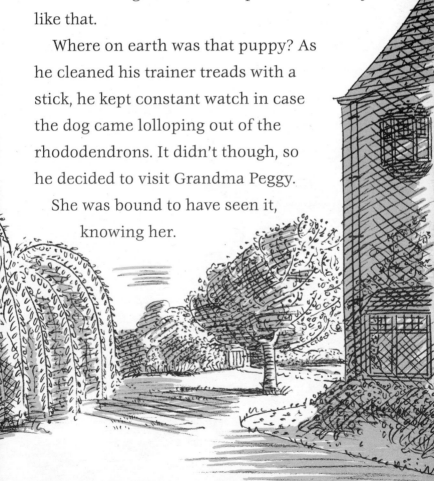

His dad would be home soon, but as his mum hadn't been around to make Grandma a cup of tea all afternoon, he decided to make her one. He also arranged some digestive biscuits on the tray with the fancy handle she insisted everyone used. He'd have rather filled it with jam ones – those were Eave's favourite – but Grandma didn't like them.

She was looking out of the French windows with a pair of binoculars when he arrived.

"Brought you some tea – what are you doing, Grandma?"

"Bird watching. Those biscuits better not be jammy ones, boy."

She claimed she hadn't seen the puppy and that dogs were a nuisance, then she put the telly on and watched the snooker. At least, she pretended to watch the snooker and so did George, but secretly, they were both keeping one eye on the garden.

After a while, George could stand it no longer and grabbed the binoculars to see if he could spot the puppy.

"What are you doing, boy?"

"Bird watching."

He saw something, but it wasn't a bird and it wasn't a dog. It was a cooked sausage on a hook dangling at the end of a fishing line that appeared to be coming down from the roof.

As the sausage got lower and lower, out of the corner of his eye, George spotted a very small,

scruffy pup looking up at it from behind a watering can.

His heart leapt. He was about to make his excuses and go after it when, without warning, his dad stepped onto the patio – only to be slapped in the face by the sausage.

Clutching his nose, George's dad watched in disbelief as the sausage whipped back up into the sky, and yelled, "Georrrrrrge!"

Chapter Seven

THATCHERS AND THIMBLES

George panicked. Without even saying goodbye to Grandma, he pounded up the three flights of stairs to his room and switched his computer on. By the time his father had caught up with him, he was busy Googling information about the care of bats. George looked up from his screen with what he hoped was an innocent expression.

"What's up, Dad? Had a nice day with Uncle Simon?"

His father scowled and pulled out a hanky.

"Sausage!" he blurted, wiping the greasy patch on his nose where he'd been swiped with the offending chipolata.

George shrugged. "You've lost me there, Dad."

His father went over to the window and pushed it wide open. He leant out, looked up at the roof, then down below. There was nothing to see – no sausage, no fishing line.

"Mind you don't fall out," said George. "You're always telling me never to lean out of windows. By the way, did you know that the pipistrelle is the smallest bat in Britain?"

His dad sat down on the bed looking confused.

"What?"

"Pipistrelles – they're the smallest bats out of all fourteen species in Britain. I'm finding out stuff so I can look after Gable properly. He's doing really well – want to see?"

Gable was still asleep, but when George tapped gently on the cardboard cage, he stirred, opened his wings then wrapped them tightly around himself again as if he were pulling a duvet back over his head.

"When I was in the Scouts..." began his dad.

George's dad often tried to tell him about the things he'd got up to as a Boy Scout. In the past, George had put his fingers in his ears, but since he'd met Lofty, he'd realized that, actually, his dad might have something interesting to say.

As his father launched into a tale about tent poles, someone tripped over in the attic. George's dad stopped mid-flow. He marched over to the green door and put his ear against it. George felt sick. Just when he thought there was no way of stopping him finding the Goffins, a bell rang violently downstairs.

99

It was Grandma's emergency bell. She kept it by the side of her bed in case there was a crisis. If she was in a bad mood, a crisis might simply be that she wanted a small sherry or couldn't find her glasses but by the sound of this bell, something much bigger had happened. Maybe she'd fallen over.

His dad ran down the stairs with George following close behind. As they got nearer to Grandma Peggy's room they could hear her shouting.

"Phil...lip! Pup's loose! Mad dog...! Dog!"

They found her standing in her dressing gown by the open French windows, waving her stick.

"After it, boy!" she yelled.

"What did it look like, Grandma?"

"Four legs, a tail, floppy ears – you know!"

George raced down the garden.

"Come on, Dad! I'll corner it and you head it off by the rhododendrons, yeah?"

Out of nowhere, the puppy ran across the path, tripped his father up then shot off in the opposite direction.

"He wants to play," laughed George. "Run, Dad. Not that way, that way... faster!"

The puppy disappeared into the bushes. George's father crawled around on his hands and knees and tried to grab it, but all he did was catch his jumper on a prickly bush, which meant he couldn't crawl back out. The pup shot off. George left his father to untangle himself.

"You stay there, Dad. I'll get it."

The chasing strategy wasn't working. It only excited the puppy more, so George walked calmly down to the orchard, calling softly. The puppy had vanished. It wasn't romping around down by the apple trees. Nor was it having a drink in the pond. He was beginning to think it must have slipped through a hole under the fence. The hole was too small for George to crawl through and the fence was too awkward to climb, so he shinned up a nearby pear tree, as high as he dared, in order to get a better view.

He clung to a stout branch and scanned the surrounding gardens and fields for a wagging tail or a flash of fur. He watched and waited for ten minutes. Twelve minutes. Fifteen. He daren't give up too soon in case Eave was watching him from the roof and thought he couldn't be bothered. No doubt Arch would have sat there all day and all night to please her, so he was just giving it another five minutes when he heard his dad call.

"George ... George? Over here!"

It was more of a loud whisper than a shout.
George scrambled down from the tree and
half-ran, half-walked over to the shed – if his
dad had found the puppy, the last thing he
wanted to do was scare it off.

"Is it in there?"

His father put his fingers to his lips.

"Shh..."

George went inside. There was the puppy,
sound asleep, curled up on what appeared to
be an old, pink baby-blanket. The blanket was
muddy and full of holes. The lace was ripped
and chewed. There were strands of elastic
bursting out of it like it uncooked spaghetti.
But it was the chewed peg stuck to one corner

that that gave it away. With creeping horror, George recognised what the puppy was really sleeping on.

"Grandma's knickers!"

The pup couldn't have been more than a few months old. It was brown-and-white with a patch over its eye and when George stroked its head, it yawned and licked his hand. He scooped it up and sniffed the velvety spot behind its ears – it smelled all doggy and warm.

"Can I keep him? Mum won't mind. Please, Dad."

His father didn't say yes, but he didn't exactly say no either.

"We'll see."

He'd have to ask Mum, but more importantly, he would have to ask Grandma.

"Grandma had a dog once. It was ever so sad, George."

"I know. But this one will make her happy – you hold him, Dad."

George pressed the puppy into his arms. His father tried to look uninterested but George knew he was melting.

They took it to show Grandma but she didn't seem very impressed.

"Stupid-looking thing. Cost a fortune to keep. More trouble than it's worth."

She picked up a magazine and refused to look at the pup. George pleaded with her.

"Would you mind him staying if I promise to keep him out of your way?"

She looked over the top of her magazine and scoffed.

"Ho! Like I have any say in my own house. Do what you like with him, boy. Just don't come running to me when he needs the vet."

George's mum came home from work. He carried the puppy into the kitchen and hoped and prayed that she'd fall in love with it.

"Oh, George. I'm not sure."

"Hold him, Mum. See? He likes you."

George's father watched her out of the corner of his eye.

She was rocking the puppy and singing the same lullaby she used to sing to George when he was a baby.

"Poor little lad," she said. "He's all alone. Shall we keep him, Phillip? It would be so nice for George and he's very responsible. Look at the way he's been caring for that bat."

His father sighed. "Alright then, but..."

"I knew there'd be a But," said George, clenching his fists. "What's the but? That I have to walk him every day? I promise I'll do it, Dad."

"But what if he belongs to someone else?"

In all the excitement, George hadn't thought of that. Nor had his mum, who was now looking sheepish for agreeing to something George might not be able to have.

"We'll ask around," she said brightly. "See if anyone's reported him missing."

"And if no one has, I can keep him?"

His parents exchanged glances and nodded.

"I'll start now." said George. "I'll knock on all the houses. I'll just check to make sure Gable's alright, then I'll go ... *yessssss!*"

He did a victory leap and ran upstairs. But it wasn't just to check on Gable. He needed to speak to Lofty and Eave urgently...

Pom ... tiddy pom pom ... pom pom!

They took ages to open the door and were very relieved to find George standing there.

"Fi! Us be afrit 'twas Pappy Phil!" said Lofty. "Myneself did trip over myne own feet most loudly. Darst say yourself be hearin' it, yay?"

"My dad heard you. If Grandma hadn't rung her bell, he'd have caught you. You have to be more careful. You know you hit him on the nose with that sausage?"

Lofty pulled himself up to his full height and looked most defiant.

"Myneself be tryin' to cotch yonder houndbubby for yourself and myne Eave!"

"I've already caught him, Lofty!" beamed George. "I caught the puppy!"

Eave jumped up and down as silently as she could, stuffing her fists into her mouth to stifle her shrieks of joy.

"Yay! Jowge be cotchin' myne houndbubby. Jowge be myne hero!"

"Wait, Eave. Mum and Dad say I can keep it, but.."

Her face fell.

"Whyfor be there a 'but' Jowge?"

He sat her down. "We have to make sure the puppy doesn't belong to anyone else."

"Pah!" stamped Eave. "'Tis myne!"

Lofty put his arm round her.

"Now, Littley. 'Tis oh-nee fair. Howfor would yourself be likin' it if somebiddy be takin' Roofus?"

Eave sat for a moment with her petticoat over her head, then she came out of hiding and demanded a piece of paper.

"Pappy, us must be scribblin' to us neighbly Goffins. Themselves might be knowin' if myne houndbubby be-longin' to somebiddy."

Lofty rummaged in his pockets and gave her an old receipt and a stubby crayon. George couldn't hardly believe what Eave had just said.

"There are more Goffins living in this neighbourhood?"

She looked at him as if he was slightly
stupid.

"Yay! Yourself be never more than five
roofs away from a Goffin, Jowge."

"Us closest neighblies be the Thatchers
over yonder," said
Lofty, pointing in a
southerly direction.
"Themselves be
livin' aloft the old
barn at Duke's Farm."

"How will you get the
note to them?" asked George.
"If I put it in the postbox the farmer might
open it. I'd take it myself but I might get
arrested for trespassing."

Lofty laughed softly. "Goffins doesn't be
needin' postin' boxes. Us uses pigeons."

Eave rolled up her miniature letter to
the Thatchers and stuffed it in a thimble.
"Chimbley will be happilee postin' it," she
said. "Come, Jowge."

George followed her to the far side of the attic where she climbed a ladder to the rafters and woke her pet pigeon, who was dozing in a pie dish.

Eave tied the thimble-letter to Chimbley's leg and when George opened the skylight, away she flew in the direction of the Thatchers.

George could hardly wait for their reply.

CHAPTER EIGHT

PUPPIES AND PEDALS

Evening came and there was still no news of the puppy's owner. None of the neighbours were missing a puppy, no one had reported one missing to the police and Chimbley hadn't returned.

Lofty said no news was good news, but even so, George didn't dare get his hopes up.

He wouldn't even give the puppy a name in case he had to give it back. He hadn't walked it because his mum said it might not have had its jabs yet, but he had played with it. He'd fed it and made it a bed in the laundry basket. In George's mind, it was already his.

He wanted to keep it in his room overnight so he could sneak it into the loft and show Eave. She was desperate to see it, but he was afraid that if he took it upstairs, it might chew the cardboard cave and upset Gable.

It was time to set Gable free. His wound had healed. He was fit and well but what if George let him go and then had to lose the pup too? To have two pets, then no pets?

He wasn't sure he could bear it.

After dinner, while his parents settled down
to watch TV, he went to speak to Lofty about
it. He found him sitting on the roof, mending
his fishing line.

George wasn't what the Goffins called sky-
savvy. He'd always been afraid of heights.
He was getting better but it still took all
his courage to climb out of the skylight. He
couldn't skip around up there like Eave did
– he was scared he'd slip and fall. Instead, he
edged his way along the roof garden on
his backside, clinging to the tiles. He
nodded to Eave and shuffled up to
Lofty to explain the problem.

Lofty listened without interrupting, then pointed to a family of bats fluttering in silhouette across the moon and said, "Yourself be knowin' what yourself must be doin'."

George's heart sank.

"I'll really miss him, Lofty. I know Gable's only a bat, but..."

"Oh-nee a bat? Lovin' somebiddy always be bringin' sorrowfill joy, be themselves bat, brother or bride, Jowge."

George was glad Lofty hadn't belittled his feelings for Gable. If he'd told his old friends Warren and Dino that he was fond of a bat, they would have probably just laughed at him and called him a wuss.

"Myneself be still a-weepin' for Whiskiss though himself be long gone," said Eave. "Whiskiss be myne mouse, Jowge. Himself be borned all nakey in Missy Violet's bonnet."

She was about to tell George
about him when Chimbley
landed on the weathercock.
Eave called and the pigeon flew
down and landed on her arm.

"Ooh ... is yourself
bringin' us news?"

Excitedly, she removed
the thimble from Chimbley's leg, felt
inside and pulled out a tiny scroll sealed with
a blob of wax.

"Aha, 'tis from the Thatchers! Pappy,
whatfor be these scribblin's a-spellin'?"

Lofty peered at the writing and wedged a
small glass lens into his eye socket.

"'Twas your Great-Grandpa Sid's monickle,
Jowge," Lofty said, tapping it.

"Don't be speakin' of monickles, be tellin'
us what news, Pappy!" insisted Eave.

Lofty shook the letter.

"'Tis ... mixed. Houndbubby be belongin' to
Farmer Duke..."

George swore loudly.

"That means I'll have to give him back.
Great – that's just great."

He could feel tears welling up. He turned
and brushed them away before Eave could
see them. He was so upset, he forgot he
was scared of heights, stood up and walked
aimlessly around the chimney stack.

"...but Farmer Duke be sellin' the litter,"
continued Lofty.

"Yay!" grinned Eave. "Jowge, yourself must
be runnin' like the wind to Farmer Duke. Do
him a Kindness and darst say himself will be
givin' us the houndbubby for free!"

George didn't need
telling twice. He ran to
his bedroom, raided his
piggy bank just in
case Farmer Duke
demanded cash,

then he got on his bike
and rode off into the night without
telling his mum where he was going.

It was a steep ride uphill to Duke's Farm.
Normally, George would have made his
parents give him a lift in the car, but now he
was on a mission. He was going to make that
dog his, no matter what it took. He would
fight Farmer Duke for it, if necessary. With
that thought in his mind, he pedalled like
fury to the farmer's cottage and knocked on
the door.

121

The Goffins Go Batty

Farmer Duke wouldn't have put up much of a fight, as it turned out. He was nearly as old as Grandma and he was already in his pyjamas. When George explained that he'd got one of his puppies, he didn't seem bothered at all.

"Oh aye?" he said. "Ah."

"Can I keep him?" begged George. "I'll pay you." He waved the ten pound note he'd got for his birthday,

but the farmer shook his head. George was desperate.

"I'll do anything – I'll weed your cornfield. Shovel cow manure – anything!"

Farmer Duke gazed up at the stars. "Yep – feels like rain. Put your money away, lad. You'll be doing me a kindness keeping the pup."

"Will I?"

"Yep."

George didn't remember riding home; it felt like he was flying. He ran indoors and shouted up the stairs.

"Mum ... Dad? Farmer Duke said I could keep the puppy!"

As soon as he could, he'd take the puppy to show Eave, but first, he had something very important to do. He went up to his room. Gable was wide awake and desperate to get out of the cardboard cave, so George lifted him up, held him to his chest and knocked quietly on the green door.

Pom ... tiddy pom pom ... pom pom!

"It's time, Lofty," he said.

"'Tis indeed. Did yourself be seein' Farmer Duke?"

George nodded. "I'll tell you about that later, yeah?"

Eave helped him onto the roof and, with a huge lump in his throat, he walked as far across as he dared. The little bat sat in his palm for a moment and washed his ears, then a gust of wind carried him off the edge of the roof like a chestnut leaf. He flittered higher and higher

until he was too far away
to see. Gable had gone.

Eave took George by
the hand. "'Tis never goodbye,
Jowge. Himself will be comin' back, yay?"

"You think so?"

"Us knows so," said Lofty. "Himself will be comin' home to roost."

They went back inside and George broke his good news. When Eave heard he was allowed to keep the puppy, he thought she was going to burst.

"When can us be seein' him, Jowge? Please be fetchin' him now!"

"'Tis late, Littley," said Lofty. "'Tis besterly if Jowge be bringin' him by morn."

She stood on Lofty's feet and fixed him with her gooseberry green eyes.

"But myneself won't be sleepin' a wink, Pappy."

Lofty sighed and gave in.

"I'll go and get him!" said George.

Just then, Eave remembered something.

"Yourself must be waitin' one tick, Jowge..."

She hurried to her bedroom and returned with Rex's old collar. The silver tag was gleaming.

"Mynself did polish it," she beamed. "For myne houndbubby."

George went downstairs to put the collar on the puppy but it wasn't in the kitchen where he'd left it. His mum and dad seemed to have gone to bed early; maybe they'd shut the puppy in the front room. George checked, but he wasn't there either – what

if it had followed him out of the kitchen earlier and wandered off? What if it had escaped into the garden when he was upstairs talking to Lofty and Eave? He'd promised to look after it – his mum and dad would be furious.

George had no choice but to ask Grandma if she'd seen it. It was late, but sometimes she stayed up to watch the boxing. He knocked on her door. There was no answer, her light wasn't on and he couldn't hear the telly, so he crept in to see if the puppy was running about on the patio. He went over to the French windows and tweaked back the curtain.

"Excuse me, boy! We are trying to sleep."

Grandma snapped on the light and there was the puppy, curled up in her arms. George sat down on the chair next to her bed.

"I was thinking of calling him Rex," he said.

She looked at him sideways.

"Not very original, but I suppose it'll do. Where d'you get that tatty old collar?"

He put it in her hand.

"A friend gave it to me. She found it in an attic. You can put it on him if you like."

Grandma read the name on the silver disc. For a while, she was deep in thought and didn't say a word.

"What are you thinking, Grandma?"

She handed back the collar.

"You put it on him, boy. He's your Rex, not mine."

"He's our Rex," insisted George. "He belongs to you, me and Ea..."

"Ea...verybody in this house!" said Grandma.

And, as usual, she was right.

Goffin Dictionary

A

a-blowin' to blow, as in wind
accibump accident
afrit scared
a-loney to be lonely
afore before
alack oh dear, alas
aloft above
appil apple

B

be-accidents by accident
be-fall to drop off, fall off
be-fallen fallen off
be-fetch to retrieve, to go and fetch
be-fix to fix an item to something
be-guise disguise
be-morn in the morning
be-nights tonight, at night
be-scribe to write
be-snuff snuff out
be-thunk thought
be-wilbered bewildered
be-yondertimes later on
besterly very best
betterly better than
bide wait
binockles binoculars
biskies biscuits
bittilee bitterly
bitwix between
blam to hit hard
blankin's blankets
blisful lovely
bloomin's knickers/underwear
boggyman bogeyman

bomb-fired blown up, as with a bomb

borned to be born

botticks bottom

bottils bottles

boudoir bedroom

bubbils bubbles

bubby baby

bulltough strong

butteries batteries

buttyfly butterfly

brainhat helmet

breakfeast breakfast

broilin' boiling

C

candils candles

carefree relaxed

chamber room

charitee kindness

cheery cherry

chickeree chicory

chimbley chimney, also name of Eave's pet pigeon

chimbley egg pigeon's egg

choclick chocolate

choon tune or song

chrizzled christened

clamber climb

clangerin' making a noise

closet toilet

clucky egg hen's egg

cockerill cockerel

coddle cuddle

cometh is coming, has come

comftible comfortable

complicockled complicated

cotch, cotched to catch, caught

cottin cotton

crafts skills

creepin' crawlin's insects, invertebrates

crumpilled crumpled

Goffin Dictionary

D

dandyloon dandelion
darst not dare not
deaded killed
deadilly dangerous
demolishin' man demolition man
dentipeep dentist
dishin's dishes
dinnin's dinner
do-long year all year
dockyments documents
does do
doin's bodily waste
doubtfil doubtful
dread fear – also dreadfill
dressin' maker dressmaker
drownded drowned

E

ebidle edible
eekwill equal
endelong lengthways
evertimes forever

F

fambilies families
fearfill fearful
feathies feathers
fi! exclamation of fear, help!
fluttermouse pipistrelle bat
foul horrid
foxsharp wily
frizzled fried
fruitibles fruit

G

gargled strangled
genteelman gentleman, polite
ghoost ghost
gnits gnats
Goffin race of people from Inish Goff, now sunk in the Irish Sea
goggils glasses

goobies gooseberries
goodly great, marvellous
grandmuppy grandma
grandpappy grandfather
grandplods grandparents
grinnin' taking the mick
grisly horrible

H

halloo hello
hamsom handsome
hark listen
has have
hastily! come quickly
hath it has
haul a fishing catch, as in a
haul of bird bread
head ouch headache
healthee healthy
hellishcopter helicopter
himself he

hither here, as in come hither
hippopottimouth hippo-
potamus
honnee honey
hooked to take, steal
horse sittle saddle
horse tack bridle etc
houndbubby puppy
hounds dogs
howfor? how can we
therefore?
hundrid one hundred

I

iggerant ignorant

J

jerkilee in a jerky manner
Jowge George
joyfill Joyful

Goffin Dictionary

K

knickybockers bloomers

L

langwidge language
larfin' to make fun of
larkswift swift as a lark
laydee woman
leaf sweat condensation, dew
lemmin'aid lemonade
lessins lessons
lionbrave fearless
littley child, kid
lo! behold
long-a-long very long
Lundiner born in London
lurgies disease

M

magifryin' magnifying
marbils marbles
meatypaste meat paste
merrilee happily, also merrimakin'
mischeef trouble
miseree misery
moffs moths

morn morning
most very
munnee money
muppy mum
myne mine, belonging to me
myneself me, I

N

nakey without clothing
nay no
neighblies neighbours
neighbourly from the neighbourhood
newspapey newspaper
niddle needle
nightlie nightie
nightly at night time
normous enormous
nutriments nourishing food

O

oh-nee only, if only
olde old
olden-day diggers archaeologists
once-a-time once
owlwise intelligent
ox-strong very strong
oziz ounces

P

pappy dad
parlour lounge
peacefill peaceful
peacefun peaceful and harmless
pedil pedal
peek to look, observe, study
peepil people
per-lum plum
piggy toe
pilloows pillows
plummet to fall
plumptious plump
plush soft
ponky smelly
'poon harpoon

Q

R

raidi-who radio
rare unusual, unlikely
rarin' urgent desire to do something now
redded embarrassed
rellies relatives
riled angry
rillytruly to tell the truth
Roamin Roman
roly-round tied
roof-fish to fish from the roof for food or items
roof legs to have no fear of heights
rumpus noise

Goffin Dictionary

S

sausagins sausages

scarifyin' to scare

screak squeak, scrape

scribblin's written matter, documents

serpent snake

sicklee ill

skrike shriek

sky-dizzy afraid of heights

sky-like skylight

sky-savvy to know how to move around a roof safely

slew kill

slippins slippers

smincey little, small amount

sniff an odour

sockets socks

softlee quietly

somebiddy somebody, usually a woman

sorely painful

sorrowfill sorry

spewerpipe sewer

spookfill spooky

springly springy

squill squirrel

squish squash

step-in sister/brother pretend sister/brother

sunsit sunset

swede suede

sweetyheart girlfriend/boyfriend

swiftlee quickly

swollied swallowed

T

tastefill delicious

terribil terrible

thanklee thank you

thus that is why, therefore

tiddlypoles tadpoles

'tis it is

to-gathered together

trash and hide to disarrange a place and remove traces of habitation

travellin' be-foots walking

trove treasured junk

'twas it was

U

uncool uncle
us we
usefill useful

V

veggibles vegetables
vessels pots etc
villins baddies

W

welly well very well
whiff to detect a smell
whumperin' whimpering
whyfor why
windyfone gramophone
windymill windmill
woe misery
Worldly War One WWI
wringle mangle
wype to wipe

X

Y

yalp yelp
yay yes
yearnin' hoping
yestertimes yesterday or in the past
yuletime winter
yonder over there
yourself you

Z

Don't miss
Lofty and Eave
in book 1

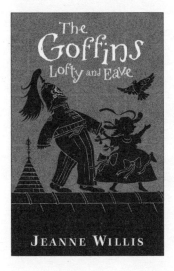

The whole summer at grumpy Grandma's house? Boring! But when George explores Grandma's attic he finds an exciting secret hidden among the moth-eaten clothes, family heirlooms and faded photographs...

He finds the Goffins!

Is there a Goffin in *your* attic?

Don't miss
Fun and Games
in book 2

The summer holidays are flying by for George and his friends the Goffins. Being left alone with grumpy Grandma isn't so bad when Lofty and Eave show him how to play spillikins, marbles and the twigaloo!

Is there a Goffin in *your* attic?